The Kingdom of
Aragon

To mason
Vivian ☺

Light your fire.
Burn it bright!
☺ yah☺

To Aiden, Our Little Fire,

You get to define who you are.....no one else. Light that fire and burn it bright:
reach high, reach strong, reach true. We are always there for you.

Love to the furthest star, Mom and Dad

HEY KIDS!

Join FRAYDO'S DRAGON CLUB!

Follow Fraydo the Dragon and Pee Wee on all their adventures!

Visit **fraydothedragon.com** to join!

littlefirepress.com

SHOUT OUTS! Thank you to everyone who has helped Fraydo the Dragon™ come to life! Special thanks to art director Anne Digges and illustration team Xi Luo & Bo Wu. To Patrick Aragon, thank you for being the Chief Sanity Officer. Gratitude to Dr. Jeremy Shumaker, who continues to help children see the world more clearly. Many thanks to our interpreter Jessie Jiang, editors Danielle Machotka and Holly Payne, librarian Susan Warnick, Sandy D'Amato at Phoenix Color, and Illustration USA art agents Stacey Endress /New York & Amary Tang/Shanghai.

LITTLE FiRE PRESS.

Light your fire. Burn it bright.

Published by Little Fire Press®
littlefirepress.com
San Francisco, CA USA

This book is not intended as a substitute for the medical advice of your child's doctor. The reader should regularly consult a pediatrician in matters relating to his/her child's health and particularly with respect to any symptoms that may require diagnosis or medical attention.

For special orders contact info@LittleFirePress.com.

Book art direction and design by Anne Digges, Digges Design, diggesdesign.com.

Printed in the United States of America by Phoenix Color, Hagerstown, Maryland.

Publisher's Cataloging-in-Publication Data

Spain Aragon, Courtney, author. | Luo, Xi, 1981- illustrator. | Wu, Bo, 1982- illustrator.
Fraydo the Dragon : a very big problem / by Courtney Spain Aragon ; illustrated by Xi Luo & Bo Wu.

First edition. | San Francisco, California : Little Fire Press, [2016] | Series: Fraydo the Dragon series | Audience: Ages 3-8.

CYAC: Vision—Fiction. | Eyeglasses—Fiction. | Contact lenses—Fiction. | Friendship—Fiction. | Empathy—Fiction. | Compassion—Fiction.

LCC: PZ7.1. S725 F73 2016 | DDC: [E]—dc23

Summary: "Fraydo the Dragon: A Very Big Problem!" is a story for children about friendship that also carries an important message about early, poor-vision detection for all parents and educators.

ISBN: 978-1-944349-50-9 (hardcover)
LCCN: 2015917453

10 9 8 7 6 5 4 3 2 1

FRAYDO the DRAGON™

woof!

A Very BIG Problem!

by Courtney Spain Aragon
illustrated by Xi Luo & Bo Wu

PUBLISHED BY LITTLE FIRE PRESS® SAN FRANCISCO, CALIFORNIA

Once upon a time, there was a GINORMOUS dragon named Fraydo.
Fraydo lived alone in a mountain cave and wished, above all else,
to find a playmate in the Kingdom of Aragon.

Fraydo often left his cave to visit the village in the valley below.
He would try to find a friend to play **Chase the Wagon**
through the cobbled streets.

The Queen
did not like
this game.

HEE HEE.
I'M WAY
FASTER!

Dear Dragon,
Do NOT
CHASE the
wagons!

Fraydo wondered why.
It was so much fun!

Dear Dragon,
Big splashes
NOT allowed!

SWEETS

PICKLES

Fraydo loved to play **Splash**
in the village fountain.

And he ALWAYS hoped a new friend
would join him.

Dear Dragon,
Big splashes
NOT allowed!

SWEETS

PICKLES

But instead, everyone always ran away.

Fraydo wondered why. It was such a great game!

By far, Fraydo's favorite game was Fetch.

He REALLY wanted a new friend
to throw his boulder for him.

But not one person would play. Not even the baker's boy.

Fraydo wondered why and became very sad.

One day, a tiny dragon named Pee Wee found Fraydo sulking by the fountain.

Fraydo saw him and asked him to play Fetch.

But Pee Wee replied, "Only dogs play Fetch.

And YOU are NOT a dog!"

This made Fraydo mad. **"I AM a dog!"** Fraydo snapped. He then stood to his full height and huffed upon poor Pee Wee, whose small wings curled from the smell.

"Whoa!" Pee Wee gagged. "You have a BIG PROBLEM!"

"Don't you see that sign the village wrote to you?" Pee Wee pointed and read it out loud.

Dear Dragon,
Big splashes
NOT allowed!

Fraydo strained to see the sign, then shook his head.

"That sign is not for me. I am a DOG!!" he barked.

"Follow me and I'll prove it to you!"

"Look! That's my **castle** up there!" Fraydo tried to make out the rocky outline of his home above the village. "Only dogs can live in castles. **Not dragons!**" he claimed.

"It looks more like a cave to me," Pee Wee grumbled.

"Humph!" Fraydo was frustrated and raced off through the countryside to find more proof.

He knocked over an apple cart
along the way.

"That's it!" Fraydo blinked hard to see more clearly.

"Over there...that's my **dog bone!**"

Skeptical, Pee Wee flew over for a closer look.

"That's NOT a dog bone!" Pee Wee squawked.

It was true. It wasn't a dog bone at all. It was an old, chewed-up wagon axle.

With one VERY upset storekeeper.

Pee Wee pleaded, "Fraydo, stop acting like a dog or you'll destroy this village!"

But Fraydo — gnawing on the axle — was too hungry to listen.

He trotted off in search of a snack that would prove he was a dog.

MMM. WHAT CAN I EAT NEXT?

"Here are my **dog biscuits!**" Fraydo drooled.

Pee Wee slapped his horns in disbelief.

"Fraydo, that doesn't prove you are a dog. It just proves **you cannot SEE** the pickle sign!"

In fact, Pee Wee thought, Fraydo hadn't seen any of the village signs.

"Fraydo, how many wings do I have?" Pee Wee asked.

Fraydo was shocked. "I don't see any wings. Don't all you forest fairies fly on **fairy dust?**"

"A FOREST FAIRY?!!!"

Pee Wee was so mad that he let loose a HUGE fire ball upon Fraydo.

Fraydo

dropped

his

pickles.

"You are a DRAGON, Fraydo!" Pee Wee huffed.

"Come with me and see for yourself."

This time Fraydo listened,
and he followed Pee Wee
to the village's eye doctor.

"Hello there!" Dr. Specs smiled.
"Do you need an eye exam?"

"Not me," proclaimed Fraydo.
"I'm as healthy as a dog can be!"

"Alrighty," the doctor chuckled.
"Let's check your vision anyway, big fella."

Dr. Specs climbed up a very large ladder.

He examined Fraydo's eyes and found the perfect lenses to clear his vision.

Then Fraydo tried on several cool-looking eyeglass frames.

Finally, his new eyeglasses were ready.

"Look in the mirror, Fraydo," said Dr. Specs. "What do you see now?"

"**A dragon! A dragon!**" Fraydo screamed.

"**Everyone run for your lives!**"

Once Fraydo got his new glasses, his world became crystal clear,

and being a dragon turned out to be a lot of fun.

Now, he could see things that were far

away like caves.

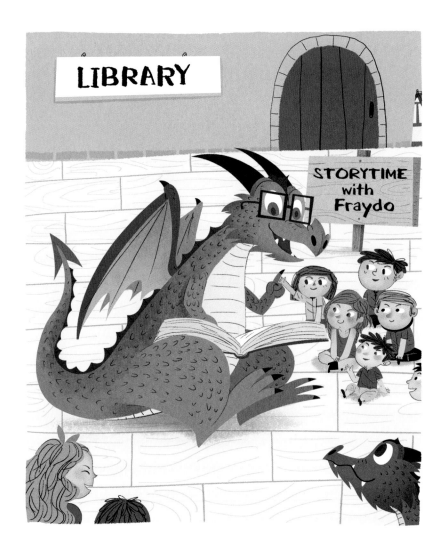

And he could see things that were close up

like signs and books.

FETCH
with Fraydo

SLIDE
OPEN

And he could play Fetch

better

than

ever!

He could see his smaller friends and
play safely in the fountain.

Best of all, Fraydo the Dragon could now see his good friend, Pee Wee,

who always had new ideas.

"Fraydo, let's fly up to your cave after our pickle snack!" Pee Wee offered.

"I can FLY?"

Fraydo was delighted.

Fraydo quickly gobbled up his pickles

so that he and Pee Wee

could start their next adventure together.